Bears Make the SCIENCE BUDDIES

written by
CARMEN OLIVER

illustrated by
JEAN CLAUDE

raintree
a Capstone company — publishers for children

Raintree is an imprint of Capstone Global Library Limited, a company incorporated in England and Wales having its registered office at 264 Banbury Road, Oxford, OX2 7DY – Registered company number: 6695582

www.raintree.co.uk
myorders@raintree.co.uk

Library of Congress Cataloging-in-Publication Data
is available on the Library of Congress website.

ISBN 978 1 3982 0197 2

Designer: Lori Bye

Printed and bound in the United Kingdom

For Declan, your curiosity always keeps us guessing. - C.O.

To Luís and João with all my love. - J.C.

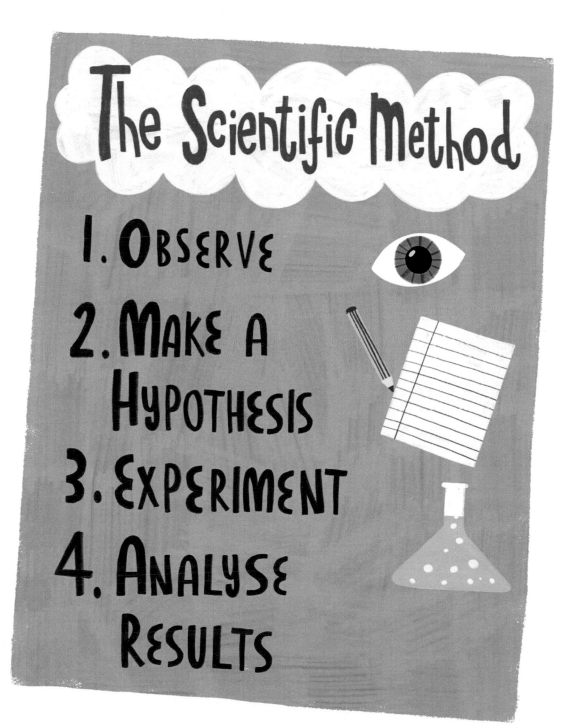

The school year had just begun, and Adelaide and Bear were looking forward to their first science lesson. But the pupils couldn't agree on the first experiment.

"Let's make exploding lava," Theo said.

"The potato clock looks fun," said Rebekah.

"I want to learn how clouds make rain," said Milo.

"What do you think, Bear?" Adelaide asked.

Bear rubbed his belly.

"I agree!" Adelaide said. "The milk and cookie dunk experiment is a great idea. You can't go wrong with milk and cookies!"

"Looks like we will need to take a vote," Mrs Fitz-Pea announced.

"Your idea will definitely win," Adelaide whispered to Bear. "Everyone loves milk and cookies."

THE GREAT MILK + COOKIE DUNK EXPERIMENT!

EXPLODING LAVA

But when everyone voted,
Adelaide's prediction was . . .

. . . wrong.

"We have a four-way tie," said Mrs Fitz-Pea.

Adelaide raised her hand. "We should draw sticks to see who gets to pick the experiment. That's what Bear would do."

"Excellent idea, Adelaide," Mrs Fitz-Pea said.
"Let's go outside."

The class gathered
sticks from the playground.

"Whoever has the shortest stick
will pick our first experiment,"
said Mrs Fitz-Pea.

Theo's stick was the shortest.

"I want to do all four experiments," he said, surprising everyone.

"Four experiments in one lesson?" Mrs Fitz-Pea said. "That's highly unlikely."

"But not impossible – especially with Bear," Adelaide said. "Bears make the best science buddies because . . .

BAKING SODA

VINEGAR

. . . they practise safety first! And whether they're in a classroom or out in the woods, bears have a wild curiosity – just like scientists. They ask all the right questions."

"And to answer those questions, bears use their five senses to observe every sight, sound, smell, taste and touch. They use this evidence to make their best guesses," Adelaide continued.

"And their pencil-sharp claws are great at recording the results and encouraging you to do the same," Theo added.

WATER CYCLE

Rain cloud experiment

		6	8
5	1	5	9
2	3		10
8	2	4	7
		7	7
6			6
		=	= 8

Theo continued, "Bears make the best science buddies because they know that every experiment leads to a new discovery."

"That's the best part!" Adelaide said. "They believe in you and will cheer you on with a big ROARRR so you'll keep going."

ROARRR!

"Is there anything this Bear can't do?"
Mrs Fitz-Pea asked.

Bear answered by moving from station to station, helping the class test out the various science experiments.

"Wow!"

"I never expected that."

"I predicted it!"

"ROARRR!"

At the end of the science lesson, Bear and Adelaide looked forward to one last experiment . . .

. . . and it was delicious.

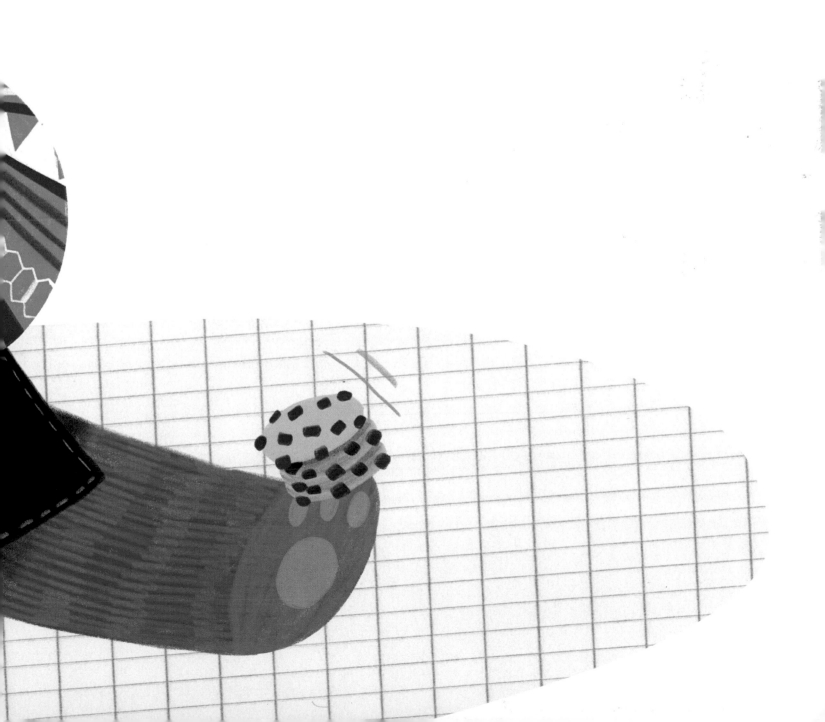

The Great Milk and Cookie Dunk Experiment

What you need:
- a notebook and pencil
- four types of cookies
- A clear glass with milk in it
- a napkin

What you do:

Step 1 (observe): Observe your cookies. How do they feel? Do some feel lighter than others? Are some thicker than others?

Step 2 (make a hypothesis): Predict which cookies you think will sink and which cookies you think will float.

Step 3 (experiment): Now it's time to dunk! Put your first cookie in the glass. What happens? Take it out and record your findings. Repeat the steps until you've dunked all four types of cookies.

Step 4 (analyse results): What is your conclusion? Did the cookies you thought would sink float? Did anything unexpected happen?